I AM N~~O~~t A

BULLY

By Paula Range

Illustrated by Paula Range

Cover picture credit to:

Canva.com

ISBN-13: 9781077247086

This book is dedicated to:

Jordan

for sitting by my side eating up every
word as I wrote each night

Natalie

for encouraging me to keep going when
I felt like giving up

Krista

for all the advice and help to get my
first book published

Rein

for helping me in the technical area
as I'm still a paper and pencil kind of
gal

Thank you to all who took time to read I AM "NOT" A BULLY and gave me their thoughts and insights...

Meagan, Izzy and Aubrey

The Nash clan

Skip and Char

Karolyn

Michelle

Mandy

April

CHAPTER 1

"Cat! Time to get up!"

"Ugh!" Groaning, I slowly rolled out of bed. "I'm coming, Mom!"

As I stood up, I looked back at my bed with its new soft fuzzy blue comforter. I had just gotten it for my thirteenth birthday, and it looked so cozy, so I flopped back down onto it. With my face buried in my pillow, all I could think about was going back to sleep.

"I hate Mondays!" I yelled into my pillow. Well, I hate Mondays during the school year. Not during the summer.

Don't get me wrong, school hasn't been too bad this year. I mean, being in eighth grade automatically made you the oldest in the school, so you were cooler than the little sixth graders. This year, I have my closest friends Holly, Amy, and Tiffany in a couple of my classes. They're all in my English class, which happens to be my favorite. Everyone calls Tiffany, "Tiff" for short. My real name is Catherine, but when I was little, I always pretended I was a cat, so my mom started calling me Cat for short. Now everybody does.

It's been a fun year, except Holly has started to get on my nerves. She got this new phone and that's been all she's talked about. She's always texting on it and bragging about it. It's the newest one out, while we all have the older versions. I really hope she'll stop talking about it soon or it could end up a very long year.

"Cat, breakfast is ready!"

Moaning, I hopped out of bed and traded my pajamas for jeans and a sweatshirt. "Yes, Mom, on my way!"

Going into the bathroom, I almost jumped at the sight in the mirror. Wow, did I need a haircut or something. My light brown, shoulder-length hair was sticking out in every direction.

"Cat, whoa! Holy cow! What the heck is wrong with your hair?"

I looked over at my sister, Grace, who was only a year and a half younger than me. "I just haven't brushed it yet."

"Well, Mom sent me up to get you because we have to leave soon."

"I know. I'm coming."

As I watched my sister twirl around to leave, I thought of how different we were. I am *not* a morning person, but Grace is always the first one up, and the thing is, she's always so happy and smiley. Sometimes her happiness is enough to make me sick. There were times when she would come in my room to wake me up and I would throw my pillow at her, but she would just smile. Good grief, it's a Monday morning and she's ready to leave already! Well, she'd just have to wait. I couldn't go to school looking like this!

CHAPTER 2

Fifteen minutes later, I found myself walking to school with Grace. I wasn't awake enough to talk, but she was skipping, and her mouth hadn't stopped moving since we left the house.

"Wow, sis, you look a lot better! Can't believe what a brush can do for a person." She babbled on with a huge grin.

"Thanks," I mumbled, still half asleep.

One thing my sister and I don't have to do is ride the bus every day. Our house is close enough to the school that we walk. Well, we walk only when it's nice out. If it's raining or really windy and cold, my mom or dad will drive us. But boy am I glad I like to walk. I've heard horror stories about the bus from my friends. They said, "so and so said this," or "so and so did that", and poor Amy has to ride for almost an hour! They also said that it's crazy loud and they always got in trouble if they stood up or switched seats. No thanks. I would rather walk to school!

As we entered the school, I headed straight to my locker to put my backpack away and grabbed my books for my first-hour class, English.

Then I heard my sister yell, "Bye, Cat! Have a good day!"

I didn't even look back. I just lifted my hand in a wave and knew that if I did turn around I'd see my sister surrounded by a lot of giggling sixth-grade girls.

As I walked into class, I saw my friends all huddled together looking over Holly's phone. "Oh boy," I thought to myself, "This could be a long day."

HOLLY: *You're such a loser! I can't believe you did that!* Send.

"Okay, guys, I sent it!"

"Great, Holly! I can't believe Trevor did that to you on the bus this morning."

"Yeah, well, he's a jerk, and I let him know it."

"Hey, guys, what's up?"

"Oh, hi, Cat. A kid, Trevor, on the bus, grabbed Holly's backpack and threw it up a couple of seats, and then laughed!" Amy said.

"Yeah, so I sent a message to let him know what I think of him."

"Okay, class, take your seats, everyone," Mrs. Hill called out.

One of the greatest things about this class was that I got an assigned seat next to Tiffany. Our desks were towards the front of the class, whereas Holly and Amy's were in the back. We don't have all of our classes together but we all meet back up at lunch.

"Class, please pay attention!"

Oops, I have a problem with daydreaming.

"I have a project I want you all to work on. Grab a partner and write down words that both build people up, and words that tear them down."

Hmm. I looked at Tiffany, "Do you want to be my partner?"

"Of course, this should be easy."

We made out our list quickly and handed it in.

"Alright, so I am going to make two columns on the board and write down all the words you guys chose."

My teacher wrote the first column, and I smiled. I saw a lot of the words I had chosen: "pretty", "beautiful", and "nice". Then she started on the side that listed all the hurtful words. I felt myself squirming in my seat. I didn't like this list.

Leaning over to Tiffany I whispered, "Hey, did you notice we use a lot of those words?"

"Yeah, I was thinking the same thing, but don't worry, we're just joking around when we say them. Plus, we don't say it to their face, so it's no big deal."

"I guess you're right, but you know Holly sends messages all the time using them."

For some reason, I didn't feel too good. My stomach started to do flips, maybe it was the blueberry pancakes I had eaten for breakfast. Or was it because we were really hurting people?

Maybe it was like Tiffany said. We're just joking around, we don't really mean it.

As soon as first-hour ended, we all headed to our next classes. When lunchtime finally arrived, we rushed to the cafeteria. As soon as we walked in, I knew it was french toast day. I could smell the cinnamon mixed with the syrup. I loved breakfast day at school. This was going to be a good lunch. Tiffany and I got in line to get hot lunch. All of a sudden, I heard a familiar voice.

"Um, excuse me."

"Hey, that's cutting! You can't do that Holly!" I heard Tyler, a boy in my grade, say.

"Well, for your information, these are my friends, and I can do what I want."

Groaning, I was afraid to turn around. I knew that Holly and Amy had pushed their way in to be by Tiffany and I. Slowly, I turned to see everyone with angry expressions on their faces, except Holly and Amy, who were grinning ear to ear.

"Holly, just because Tiff and I are up here, doesn't mean you can cut."

Pouting her lower lip, (which let me tell you, I can't stand it when she does that) she said, "You saved me a spot, Cat, so of course I can."

Looking at her with my mouth hanging open, I was just about to say something when I heard a girl, Dallas, tell Tyler to just ignore us. We were just bullies.

Bullies? We weren't bullies.

"Holly and Amy, get to the back of the line now!" Man, did our lunch lady look mad. "How many times do I have to tell you that you cannot cut!"

I thought now would be a good time to just turn around and look straight ahead. I stood there looking at the back of Tiffany's head and listened to Holly complain the whole way back.

As we were sitting at lunch, a girl who was new this year walked over and asked if she could sit with us. I was just about to tell her, 'no problem', when Holly beat me to it.

Looking the girl up and down, she said, "Um, no you're not part of our group." With a fake smile added, "Sorry."

As I watched the girl walk off, with her head down and shoulders slumped, I looked back at my friends. Holly and Amy were following the girl with their eyes, looking at her in disgust.

"That wasn't nice, Holly."

"Oh, come on, Cat, did you see her? She doesn't even look like she combs her hair! Ew, gross!"

I looked at Amy, who was now acting like she was busy eating her sandwich, and Tiff, who was too busy looking through her basketball magazine to even know what had happened. We're quite the group. There's Holly, the girly girl. She's always wearing skirts with heels. I think she's the only eighth grader who dresses up every day. Don't get me wrong, her clothes are very nice, but I would HATE to have to dress up all the time. Comfort all the way for me. Holly has always been my friend and I always thought she was so cool with her nice clothes and straight long blond hair. She sometimes comes across to others as mean, but I always thought she was just joking around, until this year. She's really starting to bug me. I can see her 'joking around' is getting worse and meaner.

Amy's like a puppy dog. She follows every word and action that Holly does, all the while, Holly eats it up. Amy tries so hard to dress and act like Holly. I just wish she would be her own self. She's a totally different person when I hang out with her and Holly isn't around. She's actually really fun. But those moments rarely happen.

Now Tiffany is more laid back and more of the tomboy. She loves basketball and doesn't seem fazed by anything. All she wears is athletic clothes. I've always loved her hair. Talk about jealous. She has this dark curly hair, the shade of her skin, but she has it sticking up with some type of cool headband. I tried one of her headbands on one time with my frizzed out crazy hair and it looked awful! I think I'll let Tiffany wear the cute headbands. She also just loves to have a good time.

Me, on the other hand, I wear what is comfy. Usually, that means jeans and a sweatshirt. I choose sweatshirts over t-shirts most of the time because

I'm always cold living in Michigan during the school year.

My friends and I have been close for a long time, but I've been struggling a little this year. Holly's attitude doesn't seem to bother my friends, but I've found that I'm becoming more frustrated with her every day. The only reason I haven't said anything to them, was because I wouldn't want them to be mad at me or not hang out with me anymore.

Maybe if we spent some time outside of school together, Holly wouldn't bother me as much. "Hey guys, do you all want to come to my house on Friday? It's only half a day of school, so we can hang out longer."

"Yeah, that sounds great. I'll have to wait until I'm done with basketball practice, though."

"No problem, Tiff, just come as soon as it's over." Smiling, my brain started running full speed on things we could do.

"Hey, Cat."

"What?" I asked, turning towards Holly.

Looking at her painted nails, a smirk slowly started to cross her face. "I was just thinking, let's all bring our yearbooks. It's been a long time since we've looked through them."

Knowing full well what that meant, I tried to give other ideas, but no one liked them.

"I like Holly's idea better," Amy added.

Of course, Amy would agree, that's all she ever did. She would agree with Holly even if she told her to run into the boy's bathroom!

"Okay," I found myself answering, knowing full well what it would mean.

Talking, laughing, and joking. All sounded fun, except the laughter and joking would not come nicely, it would come at the expense of others.

CHAPTER 3

Friday came slowly, but I was so glad when it finally arrived. As Holly, Amy, Grace, and I walked to my house, Amy asked, "Hey can we hang out in your treehouse, Cat?"

My dad had made me and my sister the coolest treehouse in our backyard. It was made of wood, with two windows. Grace and I cut out my mom's old green and white checkered table cloth to hang as curtains. We used my old fuzzy blue rug that was in my room to sit on. My friends and I have always loved to hang out in it. We've always done our nails and makeup (for fun, my mom won't allow me to wear any makeup yet). And then, of course, we've always talked about cute boys.

"Sure. I was already planning on it, but my mom said we might get some rain, so she said we need to watch for it."

"Can I come too?"

"Sorry, Grace, but it's only for eighth graders."

Rolling my eyes at Holly, I looked at Grace. I could see the hurt in her eyes. I knew she didn't like Holly, and sometimes I didn't blame her. Good grief. She's in middle school. It's not like

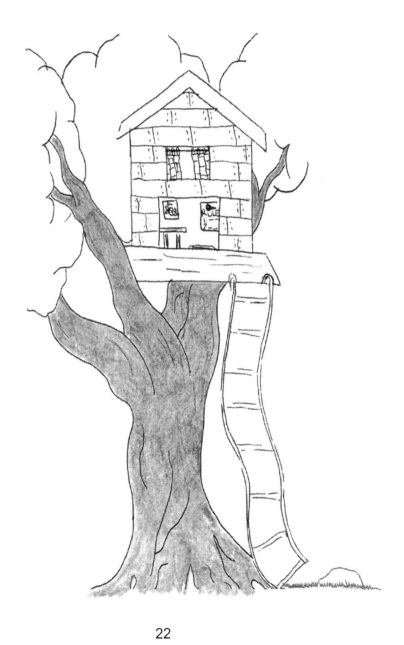

she's in kindergarten or something! I don't understand why they never want her around. Except for her being a morning person, I think she's a pretty cool sister.

Leaning over I whispered into her ear, "Tomorrow after they leave, you and I can hang out in it, okay?"

She then smiled, nodded and ran ahead to beat us home.

***

Later that day, I sat with my friends up in the tree house, eating ice cream and candy. With our hair and makeup all done, we decided to pull out our last year's yearbooks. You know, the ones with all the pictures of everyone in your class. Well, my friends and I love to look through it and point out the cutest boys, and some other things as well.

"Oh, my word! Look at this picture. Can you believe that girl, Dallas Sue?" said Tiffany.

"More like Dallas Ugly!" shouted Holly.

We all laughed.

"She used to have such long hair, and have you seen it now? She looks ridiculous! Like a boy!" Tiffany exclaimed.

"Yeah, she's in our first-hour class this year, but doesn't seem to talk to anyone," Amy added.

Holly started to flip through her phone to show us a picture that she remembered of Dallas that she had seen posted a few days ago. "Look, guys, check out her hair in this one!"

We all lean in to see her screen and started laughing.

"Can you believe how it sticks so close to her head!"

"Yeah," said Amy, "I don't know what she was thinking, but boy is it ugly!"

"Oh, I know, I know!" Holly sat up straighter with her fingers flying over the keyboard of her phone. "I'll send her a message from all of us. Hmm, what could I say?"

"Ask her if she got hit by lightning!" Tiffany said laughing.

"No! How about asking her if she got a swirly, you know where someone sticks your head in the toilet!"

"No, Amy, I've got a better idea. I know what I'm going to say," Holly said with a mischievous look in her eyes. "How about this?" She showed them her phone.

 HOLLY: *Saw you at school today. Just wanted to let you know, next time you get a haircut, if you can't afford one by a professional, then ask me for help. My dog could cut your hair better than whoever did yours! LOL.* Send.

Bursting out laughing, my friends were all talking at the same time. I started to get that uncomfortable feeling in my stomach again, but I didn't say anything because I knew it

26

was just a joke. Dallas would know we were just kidding. Wouldn't she?

"Hey, Cat, how about this picture of Tyler. I think he's kind of cute, but don't you think he's a little strange? Totally to himself. Loser!" Tiffany exclaimed.

"I know, right?" I added.

"Does anyone have him in any of their classes?" Amy asked.

"He's in our English class, dummy. Don't you pay attention? He's the one who got mad at us for cutting," Holly said sarcastically.

"How am I supposed to remember everyone in our school?"

"I know," Holly exclaimed, flipping through her phone, again. "I see him at lunch everyday sitting by himself, and he doesn't even eat his food! Here, I'll text him."

HOLLY: *Hey Tyler! See you sitting by yourself every day, and you don't even eat the food! What's wrong? Do we all make you nervous or something? Just to let you know, you could use the food, you're a little on the short side.* LOL. Send.

"Oh my gosh, that's funny! Yeah, you're right. He's probably the shortest boy in our grade."

"Guys, I don't think that matters. Plus, he can't help it if he's short." I added.

They all looked at me as if I'd lost my mind.

Finally, Holly responded, "Okay, Cat whatever you want to think."

Just then, it started raining really hard, so we got ready to pack up our things to hurry up and get into my house. As we were getting set to go down the ladder of my tree house, the rain and wind picked up till it was just crazy outside. The girls scrambled down the ladder, screaming the whole way because the weather was ruining their hair and makeup that we'd just done. I stayed a little longer, so I could put away anything that I thought the rain might ruin.

"Time to get out of here," I yelled to no one but myself. As I started to climb down the ladder, a big gust of rain and wind slammed into me and my foot slipped. Trying to grab onto the ladder, all I could feel was my body falling farther and farther down to the ground. The last thing I remembered was my head hitting something really hard, then everything went black.

Pitch black.

"Cat! Cat! Are you alright?" My head was spinning, while Tiffany sounded like she was in a tunnel far away.

All I could do was moan. My head hurt so bad, and I couldn't open my eyes because the rain was hitting my face so hard.

"Cat, it's Tiff. Let me help you up!"

"Okay." I reached my hand out, and she started to pull me up.

"Ouch!"

"Oh!" Tiffany's eyes got as big as the donut I had eaten for lunch yesterday.

"Cat, you must have hit your head on that rock. There's blood on it!"

CHAPTER 4

The rock. That must have been the hard thing my head hit. Holding the back of my head with my right hand, I let Tiffany guide me back to the house. So, long story short, my mom saw me and told all my friends to go home. Then she sent me to bed for the rest of the day.

Saturday morning came, and my mom took me to see my doctor, so he could have a look at my head. He said that I just had a nice goose egg and would need to take it easy for a couple of days. Then he added that I would probably be able to go back to school on Monday if it didn't hurt too bad. Bummer.

Once home, my mom made me stay in bed for the rest of the weekend. I just laid there and watched movies on my phone. Once in a while, Grace would come in and talk, but never for long. When Sunday night came around, my head was feeling a lot better. Shoot, that would mean I'd have to go to school the next day.

I did notice that I was having bad dreams ever since I hit my head on the rock. Hopefully, that was all that would happen from it.

***

Monday came way too quickly. Even though I liked school, it didn't mean I wanted to go on a Monday morning. I didn't want to go, but my mom made me. I tried to get out of it by saying my head hurt, which it did, but it was so much better than the days before. She told me that I was fine. I tried telling her that middle school was hard enough, and to have to go with a headache made it that much harder. She then gave me some medicine and said it would go away.

After I ran out of all the excuses I could come up with, I found myself walking into school. Nothing, let me say that again, nothing could have prepared me for what would happen to me at school that day, and how it would change my life forever. The fall from the tree house did not just give me bad dreams, it was the start of something new.

Hearing the bell ring, I hurried to get to my desk. I found the faster I moved the more my head would pound. I realized moving slowly today would be the best thing I could do. Sitting in class, Tiffany snickered and poked me in the arm.

"What?"

"Cat, look," she nodded her head towards my left. "There she is, crazy hair and all!" she whispered and then started laughing at herself.

I slowly turned to see Dallas sitting at her desk, just looking down at her lap. She must have heard Tiff's snickers because Dallas looked in our direction.

Now, this was when my life began to change. As Dallas looked over towards me, our eyes connected. All of a sudden, I started to see stars...

I see Dallas in the hospital with so many tubes poking out of her. Her doctor checks the monitors and asks her mother to come out into the hall for a minute. The next thing I know I see Dallas, lying in the bed, alone in the room. Then I look closely and see one single tear slip down her cheek. Her pale hollow cheek. She then turns over and grabs a hand mirror, pulls off her little hat and sobs. No hair at all. Dallas is battling cancer.

I gasped and leaned my head on my desk.

"Hey, Cat, you okay? You look like you just saw a ghost!"

Not even looking at Tiffany, I heard myself say, "Um, I don't feel too good."

I jumped up and ran to the bathroom out in the hallway. I started throwing water on my face. What's wrong with me? What just happened? Oh my gosh, that was scary! Was that really true about Dallas? I felt like I couldn't breathe! My chest was so tight, and I felt my throat closing up. Was I going to die? Right here, right now in the school bathroom! Sliding to the floor, I put my head between my knees as I had always seen my dad do whenever he would feel like he was about to pass out. Then I started to take deep breaths. Slowly, my chest loosened a tiny bit, and I could get air through my throat again. What was I going to do? I didn't know if I should call home and say I was sick or go back to class.

Just then the bathroom door opened and in walked Tiffany. "Hey, Cat, what's wrong?" Then seeing me on the floor, she asked, "Are you okay?"

"I'm just not feeling really good. Ever since I hit my head I keep getting headaches."

"Oh, I hope you're okay. Are you going to go home?"

"No," I said with a huge sigh, "I better get back to class."

So, we slowly walked back to class together. As I reached my desk, I just slid into my seat. I didn't want to look at anyone and have that happen again. I just looked at the floor.

"Cat," Mrs. Hill said, "Are you feeling alright?"

"Yes," I mumbled still looking down. "Just fine."

As I went from class to class, I was relieved when fourth-hour was finally ending. I knew that lunchtime always followed. So as soon as the bell rang, I couldn't get out of my class fast enough. I jumped up and headed straight to my locker. Walking down to lunch, I tried to think about what had just happened to me. The walk wasn't long enough because as soon as I walked into the cafeteria, my friends grabbed my arm and pulled me into the line for hot lunch. Taking a deep breath, I could smell the pizza. My stomach was in knots and I didn't know if I'd be able to eat anything today.

"Hey, guys," with a snicker Holly whispered, "Guess who's behind me? Should I ask her if she got my text?"

"Yeah, tell her your dog's available any time."

"Amy!" I whispered with some sternness. "Just leave Dallas alone."

"Hey, Holly's the one that brought it up. What's wrong with you anyways?"

"Nothing," I added, shaking my head back and forth to try to get rid of my headache. "I just don't feel good, and I don't think we should be teasing her. Let's just get our food and go sit down." I turned back around and started walking straight to our table while holding my tray, praying they would follow me and leave Dallas alone.

As we sat down, I could see Dallas sitting over at a table with some other kids but realized they weren't talking with her. She ate her food, then with shoulders slumped, she got up and left the cafeteria. Completely and utterly alone.

CHAPTER 5

I got through the rest of the day and went straight up to my room when I got home. I just laid there thinking about what had happened to me earlier today. What if Dallas did have cancer? My friends and I've been so mean to her. I laid there feeling awful, and it wasn't from my goose egg. I decided right then and there that I was not only going to stop teasing, but I was going to go out of my way to be nice to her. First thing I was going to do tomorrow was find Dallas and say something kind. That should be easy, just walk right up to her and say whatever came to my mind. My only problem was, what if my mind went blank? Completely and utterly blank? What in the world would I say then?

***

As I entered school the next day, I found myself really nervous. My hands were starting to sweat, I think that I made a mistake by wearing a sweatshirt today. It was suddenly too hot in the school. I didn't think it would be this hard to walk up to someone and talk to them. The problem was that my friends and I had never said anything nice to her, and for the first time, I found myself wondering what she really thought of me. Okay, I chickened out for a minute. Instead of finding her right away, I stalled and found myself heading to my locker. I saw my friends huddled together, giggling about something.

"Hey, Cat, come check this out!" Walking towards them, I had no idea what they were going to show me, but I knew it probably wasn't very nice, so I changed my mind.

"Sorry, don't have time to look. I need to do something else before class starts. Show me some other time, K?" and off I went.

As I walked away from my friends, I realized my stomach felt like it was doing cartwheels. I couldn't believe I just brushed my friends off to go and try to find Dallas. I turned down the other hall and saw her at her locker. I've never really paid much attention to her, but as I stood back to take a look,

I noticed she looked pale, small, and tired. I also could see that she had a very pretty face. She had darker skin than mine, and her eyes had a flatter look to them, and I bet if she ever smiled, it would make her face very beautiful. Taking a deep breath, I walked up to her, still not knowing what to say.

Clearing my voice, I choked out, "Hi, Dallas."

She looked around and then looked at me, not knowing if it was really me that had spoken to her. She looked down at her feet.

"Hi," she whispered so quietly I had to lean forward to hear her.

I said the first thing that came to my mind. "Just wanted to tell you I like your outfit, and your hair looks really cute today."

She just stared at me with wide eyes. Our eyes connected again, and I started to see stars. I knew I was about to see into more of Dallas's life.

It was this morning and her mom called for her to hurry up or she would be late for school. Dallas was in her room with a pile of clothes that she had been trying on but couldn't find anything that she liked. Finally, she grabbed a green top that looked pretty with her dark eyes. She then started to play with her hair that was starting to grow out, but it was at an awkward length where it was still looking like a boy's haircut. All it needed was

time to grow longer. Wiping away a tear, she whispered at the reflection in the mirror, "you sure aren't pretty like those other girls at school." Then wiping her face free of tears, she yelled down to her mom, "I'm coming!"

"Cat?"

"Oh sorry, Dallas, I didn't hear you. I was daydreaming, what did you say?"

"I said ...," with a lift of her chin she looked straight at me, "Tell your friends I don't need help from them. I like my hair just like it is." And she slammed her locker and left me standing there with my mouth hanging open.

CHAPTER 6

I slowly walked into my classroom and headed straight for my desk.

"Hey, Cat, did you see Dallas's leggings? Looks like they came off an animal with all of those zebra prints!"

Turning, I glared at Tiffany. "Knock it off! Just stop it, would you?"

Her round dark eyes stared at me in shock. "What the heck's wrong with you? You're acting so strange lately."

"Just forget it. I just don't want to talk about it." Slumping at my desk, I couldn't wait for the day to end. But the day was just beginning, and we still had lunch coming.

Later, my friends and I were sitting at the lunch table, and Holly was, of course, talking about Davis, the hottest boy in the whole middle school. He had actually talked to her. Then there was Amy eating up every word Holly was saying while twirling her long dark brown hair. She always did that when she got so caught up in a story. Tiffany was busy putting on her basketball shoes, trying to hurry through lunch so she could go off to the gym. She was the best basketball player in our grade. I just sat there thinking about what my crazy head had been doing since I fell out of the tree house.

"Hey guys, you going to come to the gym to shoot some hoops with me?" Tiffany asked as she jumped up and grabbed her ball. She always had a basketball with her. Holly, who would never touch a ball because it may break her nails answered first.

"Are you kidding? I don't want to get all hot and sweaty, and I can't play in my skirt!"

Rolling my eyes, I looked down at my tray and noticed I hadn't touched any of my food. With everything going on, I just wasn't hungry. I shrugged as I stood up and grabbed my tray.

"Yeah, Tiff, I'll shoot some hoops with you."

As soon as I stood up, I twirled around to leave, and my tray slammed into Tyler's, the boy that is in our class that Tiff had earlier said was cute but a loner. His tray collided with mine and some of our food went flying to the ground.

"No! No! I need my food!" Now on his hands and knees, I watched as Tyler scrambled to get all his food back onto his tray.

"Hey, Tyler, why do you care? Everyone knows you never eat any of your lunch anyways."

Turning to Holly, I gave her the dirtiest scowl I could come up with. I was really starting to get sick of her mouth lately. Sighing, I bent down to help him.

"Oh, that's a cute pic! Say cheese!"

I looked up just in time to see Holly take a picture of Tyler and I as we were picking up the food.

"Don't you dare post that, Holly!" I snapped.

"Oops, sorry. Too late."

I stared dumbfounded as she and Amy started laughing. I couldn't believe she just did that! Turning back around, I apologized. "I'm sorry Tyler, I didn't mean to knock your food off your tray."

"It's okay, I just need the food," Tyler mumbled as he frantically put the food back on his tray.

It was then that he looked up at me and our eyes connected.

Uh oh, here it comes again.

I started seeing stars, then the vision began...

Tyler is walking into his small canary yellow house in need of a good painting after school one day. Dropping his backpack on the floor,

he enters the living room. Knowing he needs to keep the lights low and stay quiet, he tiptoes into the kitchen and only turns on one light. He then checks to see if the couch is empty, which it is, so he heads down the hall to his mom's bedroom. Finding her covered in a light blanket softly snoring, he turns on a lamp and gently shakes her shoulder. "Hey, Mom, I'm home."

"Oh, hi, honey." She answers with slurred words, coming out of a deep sleep. "How was school today?"

"Fine."

"Just fine?"

"Yup, I'll be right back Mom."

Heading back to his backpack, Tyler then grabs a brown paper bag and brings it into the kitchen. He then takes two paper plates from the counter and lays them on the table. Opening the bag, he reaches in and pulls out his lunch from school. Cutting the burger in half, he puts a half on each plate. Next, he divides the french fries and lays them next to the burgers. Lastly, he pulls out a little container of pudding. He looks at it longingly and puts it on only one plate and adds a plastic spoon to it. Grabbing two napkins, he then walks back to his mother's room and sees that she is now sitting up in bed. Scooting over, she pats a spot on the bed where she wants him to sit.

Obediently, he sits down and hands her a plate.

"Oh, pudding today! My favorite!"

"I know Mom. Enjoy."

CHAPTER 7

I gasped! Tyler was now looking at me as if I had lost my mind.

"Oh, sorry, Tyler. You know what, though? I just don't seem to be hungry today. Would you like my food as well?"

Still staring at me, I started to transfer my food onto his tray.

"Have a nice day, Tyler." I then got up and hurried off.

"Hey, Cat! Wait up!"

I didn't turn around. I just kept walking. Holly was the last person I wanted to talk to right now.

"Gosh, you know I was just kidding. It's all just in fun. Hey, look! You already have fifty likes, just like that!"

Whipping around, I grabbed her phone and looked. Sure enough, fifty people from my school had already "liked" the picture. I looked at it more closely and saw that it was a picture of Tyler looking down, putting his food on his tray, and me looking up with a face that looked between mad and confused. I was so angry. I thought about throwing her phone into the trash as I walked by the can. Instead, I scrolled down to see what the comments were. People were actually making fun of me! I couldn't believe it! I'd never had that before. Jerks. I was already in a bad mood, and now I was in an even worse one. Why couldn't everyone leave me alone and those visions stop coming in my head? I just wanted to scream!

"See! You're the talk of the lunch hour!" Holly smirked as she grabbed her phone out of my hand.

I couldn't believe it! And she was supposed to be my friend. "Just leave me alone, all right?" I turned to head to the gym to meet up with Tiffany, but the last thing I wanted to do right now, was play basketball. Then again, with me so mad, maybe I could throw it really hard and actually make the ball go into the hoop this time.

***

As I laid in bed that night, I found my mind wouldn't let me drift off to sleep. I just couldn't believe what was happening to me. But even more crazy was how I was seeing people differently. I hadn't really cared about anybody except my friends and Grace. Now I was seeing how mean my friends were to others, and I couldn't stop replaying the visions I had been having over and over in my head.

Lying there in the dark, I thought of Tyler. Did he and his mom get their own lunch today, so they didn't have to split one? Do they ever get breakfast or dinner? I didn't know what was wrong with his mom.

Turning off the light, I snuggled under my covers to go to sleep, only my mind wouldn't stop. Was there anything I could do to help Tyler? Maybe by starting to be nice to him, or maybe just a "hi" in the hall or something. With a big sigh, I realized I was not ready to go to sleep. I wanted to help Tyler if I could. Leaning over and turning on my lamp, I grabbed my jar of savings from my allowances and counted it. I had been saving for a new phone, but I realized there was something else that I could use this money for.

With a new idea in my head, I began to form a plan. I just had to wait until Saturday to do it. Yes, Saturday would work great. I leaned over and turned off the light. Now I could rest my head back on my pillow. With a smile coming to my face for the first time in days, I sighed, turned over, and drifted off to a peaceful night's sleep.

CHAPTER 8

Saturday was finally here, and I couldn't wait to get started on my idea. I ran downstairs to see if I could find my sister Grace. Great! She was already eating breakfast.

"Hey, Grace, since it's Saturday, would you help me do something today?"

"It depends," she mumbled with her favorite cereal falling out of her mouth. "Are you wanting me to clean your room again?"

"Gross, Grace! You could have at least swallowed first!" Then smiling, I realized that my 'cleaning my room trick' was wearing thin since she was now getting older and catching on to my schemes.

"No, nothing like that. How about after we eat we go for a walk?"

"Sure!"

Grabbing a bowl, milk, and spoon, I plopped down next to her. "Pass the cereal please."

"Um, what will you give me for it?"

"Oh, come on, Grace! Just give it to me!"

Giggling, she pushed the box towards me, but when I grabbed for it, I found that it was empty. "Thanks."

Grinning, Grace stood up and went over and grabbed me a new box mom had just bought. "Here you go, but I don't know why I'm always so nice to you." She then walked off to get dressed.

Back up in my room, I jumped onto my bed and grabbed my money jar. I dumped the whole thing out onto my bed and began to count.

"What are you doing?"

"Gosh, you scared me. I didn't hear you come in. I'm counting my money."

"Do you have enough for a phone yet? You've been saving for a really long time."

"No, but I think I am going to use it for something else."

Interested now, Grace came over and sat on the bed next to me.

"What else would you use it for? It's all you've been talking about for the last, let's say FOREVER!"

Smiling, I looked at my sister, with her long brown wavy hair, so like my own. People have always said we could be twins, the only difference is that I have blue eyes and she has green eyes.

Gathering up all my money, I dumped it into a bag. I grabbed her wrist. "Come on, grab your coat. It's getting a little cold outside, and I want to go on a walk and have you help me with something. I just have to let mom know we're leaving."

Living in Michigan during October, it can really be cold. Grabbing our coats, gloves, and hats, we headed out to the garage to grab the wagon. Pulling it down the sidewalk, we had to fight off the beautiful leaves that were falling from the trees because the wind was so strong. I could hear the crunching of the dried leaves breaking as we took each step.

"Man, Grace, this crunching of the leaves sounds like you trying to eat your cereal this morning!"

"Hey!" Grace said, swatting my arm. "I can't help it that I LOVE crunchy cereal!" She then caught a leaf as it was falling off a tree.

"What color leaves are your favorite, Cat?"

"Hmm." I thought only for a second. "I love the bright yellow ones. How about you?"

"I love those too, but the orange ones I think I like best." Leaning over, she picked one off the ground.

That was how the two of us have always been. We like a lot of the same things, but we also have our differences. She's goofy and fun around people, but I've always been told I'm more quiet and serious. I've always thought of myself as nice and fun, but now I'm starting to think I'm mean, stuck up, and selfish. I hope to change that soon.

Walking to the grocery store wasn't a long walk for us. Since we live right in town, everything's close. We left our wagon outside the store and went in to grab a cart.

"What are we doing here?"

"I need to get some food. Let's see, what do you think a boy my age and a mom would like to eat?"

"Candy!"

"Grace! I mean real food."

"Oh, but could we still get some candy?"

"Well, yeah!" Then I winked at her, "And we will have to keep some for ourselves too."

"Gummies!"

"Yes, sour ones."

"Yeah, this will be so fun!"

So, after we picked out the candy (getting extra for us), we walked down every aisle. My sister and I were not blessed with being tall. Meaning, we could never reach the food on the top shelf. Grace was really getting into the shopping and wanted a bag of cereal that was way at the top.

I clasped my two hands together, and she set her foot into them and tried to stand up. The problem was, I also tried to push her up at the same time, and she went way too fast. She ended up crashing into the shelves, and before I realized what was happening, down came the cereal bag! It had gotten torn on a sharp edge of a shelf, which made it burst open at the same time the two of us went crashing to the floor. The sugar cereal exploded all over us and covered the floor!

So, what would two middle schoolers do? Well, I will tell you what we did. We laughed and rolled on the ground. Then I grabbed a handful of the cereal and threw it at Grace. That started a cereal war! We kept it up until a worker came stomping down the aisle towards us *NOT* looking very happy.

So, our shopping trip didn't just include picking out food to buy. No, we ended up holding brooms, sweeping the floor, and picking cereal out of each other's hair. Our hands ended up so sticky from the sugar, but we didn't care, because boy was it fun.

CHAPTER 9

With all the cereal out of our hair, we finally finished up our shopping and walked to the checkout.

"Keep the candy out please!" Grace blurted out to the checkout lady.

Smiling, she handed Grace the gummies. Before we even got out of the store, Grace had already eaten one

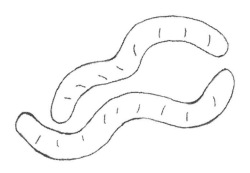

and had the next gummy worm hanging out of her mouth.

"Hey, Cat," she mumbled with the worm between her teeth. "How far do you think I can stretch it before it breaks?"

Looking back at her, I saw she had stretched the clear and red gummy till it was almost flat.

"I don't know, but I do know one thing." I snatched it from her and ran to the wagon while chewing her candy.

"Hey, that's not fair!"

Grinning, I smacked my lips. "Wow, I think that was the best gummy worm I've ever tasted!"

Grace scowled and popped one into her mouth. "Now you can't have any."

"I sure can, since I paid for them." With her holding out the bag to me, I grabbed a green and yellow one and started sucking on it.

"Okay, let's load the groceries into the wagon and head out."

As we started walking, I realized Grace had no idea where we were bringing the food.

"So, I found out that there's a kid in my class that doesn't have a lot of food and his mom is sick."

As I kept walking, I noticed Grace hadn't responded to me. Stopping, I turned around to see if she was next to me but noticed she had stopped walking and her mouth was hanging wide open.

"What, aren't you coming?"

"Hey, who are you and what have you done with my sister?"

Rolling my eyes, I started walking again. Running now to catch up to me, she yelled, "No seriously, when did you ever become so . . . so . . . NICE?"

"What?" I whirled around. "I'm nice!"

"Yeah, but you've never done something like this before. Wait, I got it, someone came in the middle of the night and took my sister and brought someone else that looks like her." Pulling on my hair, she exclaimed, "I bet this isn't your real hair! I bet it is a wig!"

"Ow, stop it Grace! Of course, it's me! I just thought I'd do something nice."

"Okay, whatever, as long as I got my gummies, I'm happy."

As we got closer to the street, I pulled out my wrinkled-up piece of paper with the address that I'd gotten off the computer. Luckily it was in walking distance from the store. If not, I would have had to ask my mom to take us. I wouldn't care if my mom had taken us, but I hadn't told her and dad about my visions yet, so I didn't know how I would have explained it to her. I told my mom I needed to run to the store and then stop by a friend's house to drop something off really quick and then head home. "Okay, the house is on this street, and the house number is 412. Help me look at the mailboxes."

"Um, Cat, is it that one?" I looked, and there amongst all the cute tiny houses was one that was in need of

some major help. The grass looked as long as my ruler at school. There were flower pots tipped over with no flowers in them. Looking at the mailbox, I saw the numbers "412."

"Yup, your right Grace. I think this is it." Now a little nervous, I eyed some bushes to the side of the driveway.

"So, what's your plan, sis?"

"Um, why don't we put the wagon behind these bushes, then let's carry the bags quietly and set them on the porch. After we're all done putting the bags on the porch, we can ring the doorbell and run as fast as we can back to the wagon and hide."

"Oh gosh, this sounds fun! Can I ring the doorbell?"

"I don't care. Just don't get caught. Run as fast as you can back to the bushes."

"Okay! Thanks, let's get started."

After setting all the food on the porch, I placed my finger over my lips to motion for Grace to be as quiet as she possibly could. Then I speed walked as fast as I could back to the wagon. I looked through the bushes and watched as Grace reached up and rang the doorbell.

Next thing I knew she was running full speed to where I was crouched down.

"Whew, that was fun!"

"Shh, let's watch. I want to make sure he gets the food."

All of a sudden, the door slowly opened a crack, next, a little farther. Soon it was all the way open. There stood Tyler looking down at the food. He then peered around but saw no one. He slowly reached down to grab the bags. On his last trip as he was closing the door, we heard him yell, "MOM! MOM! You'll never guess what just happened!"

I looked at Grace, and we gave each other a high five.

"Yes! Now let's go home, sis."

"And eat gummies all the way!"

***

Lying in bed that night, I realized how good it felt to do something nice for someone else. Sure, I would have loved that new phone, but I couldn't get one soon anyway. My parents said I had to wait until high school. I would just start saving again. Tomorrow. Right now, I was going to sleep. Rolling over, I turned off my lamp and smiled. Yup, on Monday I was going to try talking to Dallas again. Drifting off to sleep, the last image I saw was Tyler hauling bags of food into his house, while Grace watched with her eyes as big as a bagel and full of excitement.

And of course, a gummy worm hanging out between her lips.

CHAPTER 10

Monday morning came bright and early, and I found myself not dreading it like I normally did. I couldn't wait to see if Tyler acted any different today. I also wanted to try to talk to Dallas again. I actually hopped right out of bed when my mom called me to get up. I then threw on my jeans and navy-blue sweatshirt, ran into the bathroom, and got ready in record speed. I zoomed down the stairs and actually beat Grace to the table.

"Whoa, Cat, how did you get here so fast? On Mondays, I usually have to call you down about three times."

"I know, Mom, I guess I'm just a little excited to go today." Then I looked down at my breakfast, so I didn't have to explain myself.

"No way! You beat me!" Grace exclaimed, grinning ear to ear.

"She says she's just excited to get to school today."

"Oh, well that's great because maybe we won't be late for school." Then Grace mumbled under her breath, "Finally."

"Hey, can't I just be excited to go to school?"

"Yes, honey, we didn't mean to give you a hard time. It's just that your sister and I are just surprised." Then I watched my mom wink at Grace.

"You know what, girls? Since you're ready early, how about I drive you to school today? Would you like that?"

"Great! We'd love it" Grace said all excitedly. "It's been getting colder out in the mornings."

"Yeah, thanks Mom, that'd be great," I added while finishing my last bite of breakfast. Gulping down my orange juice, I hopped up out of my chair. "I'll be ready in just a few minutes. Let me know when you want to leave."

"Okay, honey." She glanced at her watch. "I think in about fifteen minutes."

"Sounds great." And off I headed back upstairs.

When I got to school, I decided to try to find Dallas. I headed straight over to her locker and saw that she had grabbed her books for first-hour. I found that I wasn't as nervous as I was last time. No, now I was actually excited. This being nice to people was kind of fun.

"Hey, Dallas."

"Oh, hi." She stuttered.

"I was just wondering how you were doing and if you wanted to hang out sometime." Thinking I was being so nice, and she would probably love to, I was shocked by her response.

"Um, no thanks." She then turned and started walking towards class.

"Hey, wait up! What do you mean, no? Why wouldn't you want to?"

With a sigh, she turned to me and spoke. "Look, Cat, I don't know why you're being nice to me all of a sudden, but you and your friends have teased me and been mean to me since first grade. I know there must be a reason you're trying to 'hang out' with me. I don't know, maybe your friends dared you and this is some kind of sick joke that will hurt me in the end. So *no thank you!*" She then turned and stomped away.

I stood there frozen like a statue with my mouth wide open. It was then that I realized the truth for the first time. *I AM A BULLY.*

CHAPTER 11

My excitement for the day had completely vanished. Yup, it was zip, zero, gone.

So, when it finally reached lunchtime, I headed to the cafeteria to sit with my friends. I asked them what they thought a bully was.

"Just a big jerk!"

"Holly, I think she means deeper than that."

"Well, Tiff, how was I supposed to know?"

Rolling my eyes, I continued, "Guys, I've always thought a bully was someone who was a lot bigger than everyone else. Usually, a boy who just liked to beat up little boys for their lunch money. But, what if it's anyone who's mean to others?" Then I paused before adding, "Let's say like us?"

"What? We're not bullies!"

"Amy, let me finish. We may not be going around punching other kids, but we say things or text things to people that aren't very nice."

"So, what? You know, and I know we're just joking around. If they can't take it, then they need to toughen up."

While Amy and Tiffany nodded that they agreed, I just stared at my friends and realized for the first time just how shallow my friends really were.

"Just forget it." I grabbed my half-empty tray and headed out. As I started walking, I ended up passing

Tyler. He looked at me just long enough for our eyes to meet, and then he was gone. I rushed over to put my tray down because I knew that the stars would probably begin. Sure enough, the stars formed...

Tyler had just brought the food we bought him into his house. "Mom! Mom! You'll never guess what just happened!"

"What baby?" Trying to sit up, his mom turned on a lamp by the couch.

"Mom, look at all this food!"

"Oh, honey, where did it come from?"

"I don't know, it was just on the front porch!"

"Well, let's see what there is." Excitement built in his mom's voice.

"Candy!" Grinning from ear to ear, Tyler pulled out the gummies. "And Mom, look! Pudding! Lots and lots of pudding. Your favorite!"

Slowly getting off the couch, his mom walked over to the table and searched through the bags. "Well, thank you, Jesus. Look at all this food!"

Tyler looked up at his mom, and her eyes began to tear up. "Oh, honey, I'm so sorry." Hugging her son, they both began to cry.

"It's okay, Mama, really it is."

"No, it's not, honey. Ever since your daddy left us a year ago, my heart has been broken in two. I quit taking care of you, and I left you to do everything. I haven't watched over you as a mama should. Instead, you've been taking care of me."

With tears continuing to run down his dark-skinned cheeks, Tyler clung to his mom with all his might. "I love you, Mama!"

"I love you too, baby."

They just held each other for a very long time, not talking, sharing sad and happy tears. Sad for how hard it'd been the past year, and for the absence of his daddy. Happy because they now had hope that he and his mama were going to be alright.

His mom finally pulled back and placed both her hands on the sides of his face and whispered, "I love you son. When your daddy left, I got really sad and thought only about myself. This show of kindness, from whoever it was, has shown me how bad I've become. I can't even take care of my beautiful son. Well, it's going to change. I will look for a job again, and you, young man," she said as she poked her finger on his nose in the same way she'd always done when he was little, "you stop bringing home your lunch to share with me. I will get my own. You, my love, you just enjoy eating yours at school with your friends."

She then took his hand and added, "Okay, who's hungry?"

"I am!"

She smiled at her son. "Then why don't we cook together this time."

I then realized that the vision was over. I looked to see if Tyler was doing what his mom said to do, and I found him eating his lunch for the first time this year. Instead of with friends though, I noticed he was sitting at the table all alone. Tyler had no friends.

CHAPTER 12

With school over for the day, I found myself lying on my bed in my room just staring at the ceiling. I didn't know why I kept seeing into other people's lives. What in the world was I supposed to do? Why couldn't I be normal again? I just wanted to tell someone. But who in the world would believe me? I couldn't tell my friends. They would tease me and say I'd gone crazy.

Oh my gosh! A thought occurred to me. I sat up in bed and said out loud, *"What if I am going crazy? What if I'm never normal again?"*

Okay, I could tell that I'd started to panic. I *had* to tell someone. Maybe I could tell Grace. Just then, my bedroom door swung open with a vengeance, and she came barreling in.

"Cat! Cat!" Running in, Grace jumped onto my bed a little too hard and flew right off the other side.

"What are you doing?" I asked, half laughing. I couldn't tell if she was laughing or crying.

"Oh my gosh! That was so fun! Did you see me just flip right off your bed?" She was laughing so hard, I started to get nervous that she was going to pee her pants. She had always been one of those people who wouldn't be able to hold it in if they got laughing too hard.

"Stop laughing or you might pee on my floor!" I added, laughing now myself.

"So... so.. sorry, Cat! I just came in to see if you talked to Tyler today. If you did, did he say anything about getting the food, and if he liked it? I am ..." And then the laughing started up again. She was still laying on my floor, until she jumped up, "Oops! I have to go to the bathroom!" She then raced out of my room.

I yelled after her. "You better not have peed on my floor! Gross!" Smiling, I realized she was one crazy sister, but that's why I loved her.

After a few minutes, she came back into my room with a different pair of pants on. "Oh really, Grace! You better not have gotten anything on my carpet!"

She then smiled and added, "No, I think I peed on the way to the bathroom, but you know how it is. Sometimes you just can't stop laughing!"

Smiling back at her, I asked her to sit down. "Okay, I have something to tell you, but you can't tell anyone, and you might not believe me."

Her smile left her face. "Of course. What?"

"Um, do you remember when my friends came over a few weeks ago?"

"Yeah."

"Well, do you remember when I fell out of the treehouse when I was climbing down the ladder? It was raining so hard and the wind had picked up and my foot slipped. Then when I landed, my head hit a rock."

"Oh yeah, I remember Mom taking you to the Dr., and you kept saying you had a headache."

"Well, it did something to me."

"What did?"

"When my head hit the rock, it did something to my brain or something."

Grace laughed. "Well, I could have told you something was wrong with your brain a long time ago."

"No. I'm serious. I.. I.. I can see things."

"See what?"

"Um, kinda into people's lives, visions or something."

Grace just sat there and didn't say a word. I didn't know if she thought I had more to say, or that she had no idea what to say.

So, I continued. "If certain people look at me, and our eyes connect, I can see things that have happened in their lives before."

Grace slowly leaned towards me and opened her eyes as wide as she could until our noses were almost touching. "Can you see anything? Can you read my mind?"

I pushed her away. "See, that's why I didn't know if I could tell you. You're teasing me."

"No, sorry, Cat. I guess I don't know what you mean."

"Well, remember how we shopped for Tyler? The only way I knew that they needed food was from me seeing a vision of him at his home. He was sharing his lunch with his sick mom because they had no food."

Sitting there now wide-eyed, Grace whispered. "No way! Can you see everybody's lives?"

I shook my head in confusion. "No, that's what I don't understand. I only see people who are hurting." Not wanting to add the last part, I quietly added, "I think it's the people who I've teased and hurt in the past."

"Well, then you should see into my whole life!" Grace added trying to lighten the mood. She had always done that. She never liked to feel uncomfortable. "You have always teased me!" She then winked at me and gave me a hug. Whispering in my ear, she added, "Your secret is safe with me. I won't tell anyone."

"Thanks." I hugged her back. "You're a great sister. Just don't let it go to your head."

Leaning back, she smiled, but it didn't last long. "You know, sis, will you promise me something?"

"Depends on what it is."

"Will you tell me when you see the visions, so I can help them too?"

Thinking it over in my mind, I answered, "You know what, I can't promise you that I'll tell you all the visions, because I don't think these people would want this stuff known, but I will tell you any time I think we could help one of them."

"Thanks, we'll be our own little team." She jumped off my bed and started to leave.

I threw my pillow smack on the back of her head. "And next time, don't pee in my room!"

CHAPTER 13

Back at school the next day, I looked around and saw that Tyler and Dallas were both in class today. Maybe I should try to talk to them again. Would I get another vision from them? I looked their way, but they were both looking down at their desks.

"Okay, class, today I want you to all work on a project. The project is going to take all week to work on. I will be giving you the hour each day during class."

Tiffany kicked my foot, "Partners?"

"Yeah."

"Now, the thing is, I'm going to pick your partners this time."

I whipped my head toward Tiffany. "Looks like we might not be partners."

"Hmph, that's stupid."

"It will be fine." I was kind of hoping I would get with Dallas or Tyler. I know Dallas doesn't like me, but I wanted her to know I wouldn't be mean to her anymore.

As Mrs. Hill called off names, I heard that I was paired up with Becky. Oh, I quietly let out a little groan. Becky was kind of different. She would try talking to everyone in the class as if we were all best friends. Why couldn't I have gotten paired up with someone else? I looked over, and she was smiling from ear to ear, looking straight at me. Now there was a girl that you could never hurt. She had been teased since kindergarten because she was so much bigger than everyone else. I think she's probably the fattest of the whole middle school. But the mean words never hurt her, she just smiles and talks to everyone.

Snickering, Tiffany whispered, "Have fun."

Remembering that I wanted to act nicer to people, I sat a little taller, lifted my chin up a little higher, and heard myself saying, "I will have fun. Becky is nice."

With a shrug, Tiffany turned and stood up. "At least I got paired up with a cute boy."

I watched her walk off, and I turned around to find Becky walking towards me.

"Hey, Cat, can you believe we're partners? This will be so much fun!"

Giving her my best smile, I said, "Oh yeah, it will be great."

"Do you know what the project is supposed to be?"

"No, I think she will explain it to all of us soon, why don't you sit at Tiff's desk and wait to see what she says."

"Now class, here's the project. I am going to ask a question, and you and your partner have one week to answer it. I want you to make a poster with pictures to go along with a one-page report explaining your answer and what you are going to do with it. Here is the question. *If you won one thousand dollars, what would you do with it?*"

"Go shopping for shoes!"

"Holly, you and your partner will have to agree on what you spend it on. I don't think Connor will want one thousand dollars' worth of shoes."

"Well, what if we don't agree?"

"You're going to have to come up with something if you want a good grade. Now I'll give you the next hour to work on this project. It will be due one week from today."

"One thousand dollars!" Becky exclaimed. "Can you imagine, Cat? That's a lot of money!"

"Yeah, do you have any idea what we could use it for?"

Becky started pulling out a pad of paper and grabbed my pencil. "How about we just start by writing down ideas."

"Okay. Sounds great. Um, I have an idea. We could get some really cool cell phones!"

Smiling, Becky wrote down "cell phones."

"Oh, I got one! How about we throw a big party, with lots of balloons and food!"

"A party?" I was just about to tell her that was kind of a dumb idea because why would we want to spend our money on balloons when we could get new cell phones. As I opened my mouth to tell her what I thought, she looked straight at me with wide eyes full of excitement. Our eyes connected. I started seeing stars...

"Becky, are you done hanging the balloons for your birthday party?"

"Almost, Mom! Can you believe I'm six years old today?"

As Becky's mom walked over, she bent down to give her daughter a hug. "No, sweetheart, I can't believe it. You have grown up so fast. Just please stay my little girl a little longer. "

"Oh, I will Mom. Don't worry. I'm only in kindergarten."

Giving her daughter a kiss on her chubby little cheeks, she said, "Okay, honey, your party starts soon. I have the cake and punch ready. Now you finish hanging the balloons."

"Yay!" Jumping up and down, Becky ran in the middle of the room and lifted her head up, arms stretched out, twirling around in a circle. "Mommy, my first birthday party. I'm so excited!"

Smiling, she said, "I know, honey, and you invited your whole class. This is going to be a big party!"

"Yes!"

A while later Becky leaned against the back of her couch, looking out the front window. "Mommy, what time is it? When will they all be here?"

Her mom looked at the clock with a worried face. "Um, soon. They must just be a little late."

TICK-TOCK, TICK-TOCK, TICK-TOCK

With cake untouched and balloons deflating, Becky's mom went over to the couch. It was now dark out and time to put her precious daughter to bed. Lifting the sleeping child into her arms, she studied her daughter's face. Beautiful, with round rosy cheeks, blond wavy hair, but what broke her mother's heart the most, were the dried-up tear stains on her daughter's cheeks. Lying her in her bed, Becky's mom covered her sleeping child and kissed her goodnight.

"Night, night, sweetheart, and happy birthday. I love you so much."

As she started to walk out of the room, she heard a quiet tired voice. "Mommy?"

"Yes, dear?"

"Why didn't anybody come to my birthday party?"

Leaning against the doorframe, her mom sadly replied, "I don't know, honey. They must not realize what a great friend you are."

With a sniff, Becky replied, "At least I have my balloons," and rolled over and went back to sleep.

I blinked my eyes a couple of times and looked at her.

"So, Cat, what do you think about the party idea?"

When I finally found my voice, I heard myself say, "Yeah, a party is a great idea, and the more balloons, the better."

Chapter 14

The next day, Becky and I worked together to come up with our plan for our project. At first, we thought of a lot of different ideas, but we finally narrowed it down to two.

"Okay, Cat, so we are either going to have a big garage sale and the money goes to help the kids in our school or the homeless. How do we choose which one?"

"Hmm, I don't know, because I think they're both great ideas."

I looked over and saw Holly across the room cutting out dressy shoes from magazines and Conner gluing them on a poster board. Shaking my head, I realized that I was glad I got paired up with Becky. The more I got to know her, the more I realized how nice she was, and how she always thought the best of everyone else. I looked back at her with a thought. I remembered how old Tyler's backpack was in the vision I had of him.

"Becky, I know there are kids in this school who don't have a dinner to eat at night and some probably need backpacks. What if we helped them from our sale?"

"That sounds like a great idea, and even though we'll do a sale, we can still decorate it like a party."

"Definitely! We could do it in the cafeteria or gym and get balloons and streamers! We could use some of the money to buy the decorations, but the rest to help go towards the kids!"

With both of us excited and wearing huge grins, we got out our markers and started to work on our poster.

By the following week, we had already worked really hard and gotten most of it completed.

"Class, tomorrow we will start having each group come up and read their paper and show their poster. I am going to invite the principal to come in to listen to them also, so be ready."

"Oh, man, the principal is coming. I sure hope he likes our project."

"Of course, he will, Cat. I think it's wonderful."

"You know what, Becky? I think you're right. It really is a great project! You sure had a lot of great ideas, and I am sooo excited to tell Mrs. Hill about it tomorrow."

***

Today is the day. I can't wait for our turn. People have been giving their reports, and so far, no one has had our idea. Holly is up front with Conner right now talking about spending her one thousand dollars on shoes. All the different styles and colors.

"You can never have enough shoes!"

Clearing her throat, Mrs. Hill cut in, "Well, thank you, Holly and Connor. It was very, um, let me say, interesting. I do want to know though, Conner, why did you agree to go along with this topic?"

"Well ..." We could see his face turning a little red. "Holly promised me candy if I did the project on shoes."

The room went silent, then I heard some snickers. Everyone was staring at Mrs. Hill to see her reaction. Holding our breaths, we all waited to see what she would do. Would she be mad, laugh, or not care?

"Go take your seats, you two. *Now.*" And boy, did she not look happy.

It was now our turn. We grabbed our poster board and walked up to the front of the classroom. I had never been good at talking in front of the class, so I was so glad when Becky started to do the talking.

"So, we thought about using the thousand dollars to have fun, but to help others at the same time. We would have a huge sale at the school selling our stuff from home. We would take the next few weeks to collect a whole bunch of items and then sell them. The money would all go to kids at this school that don't get a dinner at night or need a backpack or some clothes."

"Yeah," I added. "We would decorate it like a party and have music playing in the background."

"And," Becky chimed back in, "we could sell food at it too! It would be so fun, plus we'd be doing it for a good cause."

"How is that fun for you?" Amy yelled out. "You said it was fun, but it sounds like a lot of work, and you don't even get to keep any of the money."

I looked at Becky to see if she was going to say anything or if she wanted me to.

"The fun for us is throwing the party. I love parties, and knowing we are helping others our age makes a person feel good."

"Sounds like a lot more work than fun to me," Holly chimed in. "And honestly, I would have to agree with Amy. I would consider doing the sale if I could then use the money to go shopping."

"Well, girls," their principal said, "I personally love the idea!"

"Thank you, Mr. Holman."

"You're welcome," he said with a smile.

"Okay, class, I really liked everyone's reports, but I would like you all to put your stuff away and grab a book to read while I step out in the hall with Mr. Holman for a couple of minutes."

"Thank you, Cat, for being my partner. I had a great time."

"I know. Even though it was just a project, I got really excited about it. Thanks for all your ideas."

"Yeah, well time to read." She walked off, making a funny face and mumbling, "Yuck, I hate reading."

Smiling, I turned to go back to my desk and realized how much fun I had this past week with Becky.

"Hey, Cat."

I looked at Tiffany. "Yeah?"

"Did you make it through the week having to work with you know who? I bet you were dying!" Laughing at herself, Tiffany snorted in a way she did whenever she laughed too hard.

Now I was getting mad. "No, Tiff, I wasn't dying. I actually had a great time with her." Feeling kind of bold, I added, "And you know what? It was nice hanging out with someone who wasn't teasing or mocking others the whole time."

Tired of it all, I just wanted to go home, but we were only in first hour. I grabbed my book and opened it to where I left off last time. I looked at the pages, but I couldn't seem to concentrate on the words. I was so tired of everyone being so mean, myself included.

Our teacher and principal came back into the room and walked up front by the chalkboard. "Okay, class,

Mr. Holman and I have a surprise for you all!" Clapping her hands together, she looked at the principal.

"All right, kids, your teacher came to me a couple weeks ago with her idea for this project. Together, we came up with an idea to continue the project."

"No!" Conner cried. "I can't take any more days hearing about shoes! I thought we were done." He looked at Holly and added, "You owe me more candy!"

Smiling, our teacher stepped forward. "No more shoes, Conner, don't worry. But what we want to say is that it doesn't end here."

"Your teacher and I listened to all of your reports. They were all very good, but there was one that we thought stood out from the others. It was a wonderful idea."

"Cat and Becky, would you two please come up here?"

Looking around, I must have looked confused, but Becky was just a grinning. As we went up in front of the class, we looked at our teacher and then to the principal.

"Girls," Mrs. Hill said, "I had invited Mr. Holman to listen to the reports. Then, we decided if we thought there were any that were worthy of being done in real life. And we chose yours. The school is giving us one thousand dollars, and we are going to do your idea and have a sale to help kids get food and items they need."

"What? No way! Mrs. Hill, are you serious?" Becky cried out as she hugged our teacher.

"Yes, Becky, we are very serious. We really liked your idea. Now, you two need to pick two other people in the class to work with you over the next couple of weeks to help you get it all organized. Then we will all help and be at the party with you."

I saw Becky crying. She was so excited. I whispered to her, "Who do you want to pick to help us?"

With her hands over her face, trying to stop her happy tears, she mumbled, "I don't care."

I lifted my eyes and looked out at the class, and I heard myself say, "We would like Dallas and Tyler to help us please."

At that very moment, the bell rang, so I turned and headed out of the room, but not before I noticed Holly, Amy, and Tiffany scowling at me, while Dallas and Tyler's mouths were hanging open.

CHAPTER 15

The following Monday, I got ready for school and headed out with Grace. I was so excited to talk to Becky. All I could think about the whole weekend was the project. I couldn't wait for today to come so I could tell her some ideas I had. We only had two weeks to get it organized. When I finally got to school (seemed to take extra-long this time), I headed straight to my desk to put my papers away. That's when I heard, "Traitor!"

I looked over to see Holly, Amy, and Tiffany all standing by each other, arms crossed scowling at me. All of a sudden, it felt like the room was getting hot, or was it just me? I looked around to see if anyone else was sweating. Nope, I guess the girls were making me nervous. They had started walking my way, but just as they got close to me, I saw Becky standing in front of me.

"Hey, Cat! I got some ideas about the party. Can we talk at lunch?"

Looking at my friends, who were now standing behind Becky with faces that were not very friendly, I turned back towards Becky and answered, "Um, yeah sure, I have some thoughts too."

"Great! See you at lunch!" As Becky walked away, my friends stepped towards me.

"Did I just hear you say she can eat with us at lunch?"

"Well, I just need to talk to her about the party."

With her arms crossed Holly said, "Well, she's not allowed to sit with us, so what do you say about that?"

"Wait, are you making me choose between you guys and her?" I felt like I was in an oven. My face was burning, my hands were sweating. I wondered why no one would open the windows.

"Yeah, that's what we're saying. When lunchtime comes, you choose who your *real* friends are."

Holly then twirled around while Amy and Tiffany followed her back to her desk. For me, I plopped down into my chair, knowing lunch would be here soon, and I had to make a decision. A hard decision.

***

Walking with my tray at lunch filled with a burger and fries, I looked around and saw my friends since kindergarten at a table to my right. Then at a table to my left was Becky, Dallas, and Tyler. Becky waved her hand in the air. "Over here, Cat!"

I looked over at Holly, Amy, and Tiffany, and they just stared at me, probably waiting to see what I was going to do. With a big sigh, I made my decision. I turned my back to my friends and walked towards Becky. She had no idea how hard this was for me, because I may have just lost my friends.

"Hi, guys," I mumbled as I sat down.

Dallas and Tyler looked just as nervous and uncomfortable as I felt. Becky, on the other hand, didn't seem to notice. She was just so excited. "Okay, I've got some ideas."

For the next half hour, we threw around different thoughts. By the time lunch was over, we realized we had a lot more to talk about.

"Hey, guys, why don't you all come over to my house tomorrow, and we can do more planning." It went dead quiet. I didn't know what I had said wrong. "What?"

Dallas spoke first. "You are inviting us to your house?" They all looked at me kinda funny.

"Well, yeah, that's what I said."

I then heard Becky quietly choke out, "Me? Come to your house?"

What was wrong with these people?

"Of course. Is there something wrong with that? I mean, we can go to one of your houses if you would rather do that."

For the first time, Becky was speechless, and I could see her eyes get a little misty. Then our eyes connected. The stars started to come again...

I saw Becky at her house watching TV and her mom came over to her, sat on the couch next to her, grabbed the remote, and clicked off the TV.

"Hey, honey, can we talk a minute?"

"Sure, Mom."

"Well, I know it's Friday night, and I thought you said some girls were having you and some other kids over."

Looking down at her bowl of ice cream, she responded, "Yeah, well, it didn't go as planned." Then putting on a smile, Becky said, "But it's okay, Mom. Really don't worry."

"Honey, did you get invited?" Focusing her eyes back onto her ice cream, Becky replied, "No, Mom, they didn't invite me."

"I'm so sorry. I know you really wanted to go."

"It's okay, Mom. Really, I don't care. You know I've never been invited to anyone's house before, so it's no big deal."

Trying to understand her daughter, her mother asked, "Becky, how do you do it? How do you always smile when you have people say mean things to you or don't invite you to anything? Why do you keep on smiling?"

"Easy, Mom. I smile to not let them know my true feelings, because if I don't smile I will break down and cry."

And that is what she did. Her mom leaned over and gave her a loving hug and let Becky's tears flow.

Staring at them all, I said quietly, "Yeah, I'm inviting you all to my house tomorrow, would you like to come?"

"Yes!" Becky almost yelled. "I would love to come to your house!"

Smiling, we all walked back to our lockers together.

CHAPTER 16

Saturday came, and I got ready for them to come over. I had told Grace last night who was coming, and she got real excited and wanted to make brownies for them. Now Grace has always looked for an excuse to bake, and when she does, it's so good! She's always been the one helping my mom in the kitchen making dinner, but her favorite has always been baking desserts.

Just this year, she started making some on her own without my mom's help. When she says she will make brownies, they're not your average normal brownies. No, they will have a cup of chocolate chips in them, topped with frosting and sprinkles.

As I was helping her put the final sprinkles on, someone knocked at the door.

"They're here!" Grace yelled, "I hope they like my brownies!"

"Oh, I know they will." I said as I licked the last of the buttercream frosting off my fingers.

As I walked to the door, I yelled back to my sister, "Hey Grace, if you want, you can hang out with us. You're the artsy one and might have great ideas that can help us." I then took a peek behind me and saw that my sister's smile traveled from one ear to the other.

As I opened the door, there stood Becky and Dallas. After inviting them in, I was just about to shut the door when I saw a tan car pull up. Out jumped Tyler, and I looked to see his mom rolling down the window, yelling out to him. "Have fun, honey. Just call when you need me to pick you up."

"Okay, Mom." Tyler looked up at me with his dark face and deep dark eyes. They had the look of embarrassment.

Trying to help Tyler not feel uncomfortable, I waved at his mom and then turned to say, "Well, you sure have a nice mom."

He turned back around to watch his mom drive away. "Yeah, I sure do."

"Come on, let's get started."

As we walked back into the house, I heard Becky talking about how good the brownies tasted and how cute they were. I looked at Grace, and she was just beaming. After today, her smile may get stuck in that position.

"Thanks, Becky, I do love making them, and Cat helps me."

"All I help you with is tasting the batter and decorating. You do all the baking."

"Wow!" Tyler exclaimed as he bit into one. "These really are good!"

"Hey, Grace, would you like to make these for the party we're planning?"

"Sure, Becky, I'd love to!"

"Good! But we'll need a lot of them, can you do that?"

"Tell me how many, and I'll have them ready."

"Okay, guys, we're all here, so let's get started. We have a lot to do in two weeks." I said, getting excited myself.

The late afternoon ended up flying by, and the next thing we knew, it was time to wrap it all up.

"I think we've got it. Thanks for coming over."

"Yeah, thanks Cat for asking us to help. It really was a lot fun. I don't know when I've laughed so much."

"Me too! My stomach hurts, and I don't know if it's from eating too many of Grace's yummy brownies or if it's from laughing so hard," Becky said as she grinned so big her eyes were almost closed shut.

After we said goodbye, I shut the front door, and Grace stood next to me with a look of complete happiness.

"Wow! That was so fun. They're so nice. Thanks so much for letting me hang out with you, sis."

"Any time. You were a great help." I then started walking up the steps to my room, thinking about the day. I realized for the first time that we had so much fun and none of it was by teasing or talking bad about others. No, it was deep down, belly laughing fun.

**

As it got closer and closer to the day of the party, I found myself hanging out with Becky, Tyler, and Dallas more than with my other friends. They weren't being very nice to me now anyways. I think they were really mad at me. I still talked to Tiffany sometimes because she sat right by me, but she didn't seem very happy with me, and Holly and Amy wouldn't even speak to me.

"Okay, class, the party is this weekend. Cat, Becky, Tyler, and Dallas have worked so hard on this that I would love to see if you could all come to it. They could use your help working the sale. It will be this Saturday at 9 a.m. They have already put flyers up, and we hope to have a lot of people come. Cat, were you able to collect a lot of items for the sale?"

"Yes, we have car loads of all different kinds of stuff. We can't believe how many people donated things for it." Pausing, I asked, "Mrs. Hill, we're just wondering if we could maybe use Friday during school to decorate and get ready?"

"Yes, definitely. Now let's go over the details one more time to make sure we all know what we're supposed to do."

As we went over all the details, we realized we still had to buy all the decorations, so Becky, Tyler, and Dallas decided to meet up at my house after school later today. We needed to get the balloons, tablecloths, and food. We all decided it would be a good idea if we sold Grace's famous brownies. Becky kept raving about them and said she could probably sell about five dozen of them. I went on to tell them that she makes awesome chocolate chip cookies too, so they suggested that she sells those also. I couldn't wait to get home to tell her.

***

A few hours later back at home, I heard Grace yell, "They're here! They're here!" as I watched her fly down the steps. Taking a whiff of something good, I realized Grace probably made up some of her cookies. She must have done it after I told her they thought she should sell some at the sale. Smiling, I followed her and realized how much fun I had been having with her since I'd started hanging out with these other people.

My other friends would have never allowed my sister to hang out with us, but these guys not only didn't mind, they encouraged it and asked her to hang out with us. Grace was planning on going shopping with us later today, and when I talked with her, she was so excited to help out at the sale too. The whole group had loved having her around the past week, and I realized that I loved it just as much as they did.

"Come in, come in," Grace greeted them at the door.

"Hey, do I smell cookies?" Tyler asked.

"Yeah, chocolate chip ones. Cat said I could bring some to the party to sell, so I thought I'd make some up and have you guys try them to make sure you think they're good enough."

"Thanks Grace, you're the best!" Tyler lifted his hand to give her a fist bump.

"I'm so happy that my sister loves to bake because I would totally mess it up. One time, I tried to make a cake and the outside edges were all hard as a rock, but the middle of the cake was all goopy. I don't even know what I did wrong. Luckily, Grace not only loves it, she's so good at it!"

"Well, then I'm glad Grace made these ones." Dallas said with a little smirk.

We all decided to sit around the table to eat some of the cookies with milk before we headed out to go shopping. I sat back and just listened to them all talk. There was so much laughter and smiles going around the table. Wow, was this so different than my get-togethers with Amy, Holly, and Tiffany. This time, there was no ripping on others or tearing people down.

I found myself just fascinated with watching them all. This was so much more fun. These people around the table were not at all part of the popular group, and actually they weren't part of any group. They all struggled fitting in anywhere, but looking at them now, it seemed like they had truly found friends. I've gone to school with them since kindergarten and have always looked down on them, but now they're in my house, sitting at my table, eating cookies, and having a ball.

Guilt started to settle in, and I started to feel really bad about the way I'd treated them in the past, but it didn't last long. They didn't give me a chance to get depressed, because before I knew it they were jumping up from their chairs and getting ready to go.

"Come on, Cat!"

I felt a hand on my arm trying to pull me up. I looked up and saw that Becky had a smile on her face that was as long as the Mackinac Bridge.

"No time to be frowning, this is going to be so fun!"

Letting her drag me out of my chair, I felt all the guilt evaporate, and I couldn't help but smile.

"Okay, let's go!" I found that I was just as excited as they were.

"Were leaving, Mom!"

We faintly heard my mom calling back, telling us to be careful but to have fun. We talked and laughed all the way to the store. Dallas kept trying to ride in our wagon as Tyler pulled her. The leaves and acorns on the sidewalk slowed them down so much that she ended up having to get out and walk.

CHAPTER 17

As we entered the store, I heard Grace telling them about our cereal incident the last time we were here. I scowled at her because I didn't want Tyler to know it was us who had given him the food. Luckily, she didn't say why the two of us had been shopping. As she finished the story, she looked over her shoulder at me and winked.

"Okay, guys, let's find the balloons!" Becky took off full speed ahead.

We all looked at each other, then Dallas said, "Well, you heard her guys." With a grin, she added, "Now let's go!"

And off we all went in search of balloons.

A little over an hour later, we left the store with arms loaded with goodies. I found myself having so much fun walking back towards my house as I pulled the wagon with decorations and treats for the sale. We all had our favorite candy in our mouths. Each one of us had picked a different kind, but of course Grace was busy talking a mile a minute while she played with a green and yellow gummy worm, which was dangling between her teeth.

After we got back to my house, we all decided to go up into the tree house.

It was a nice fall day, not too hot and not too cold.

"Wow this is a cool tree house, Cat!"

"Thanks, Becky. Grace and I love it up here."

"Yeah, but I never get to join her when she's with her *other* friends. They won't let me up here."

"What! Why not? You're so fun!"

Grinning, Grace hugged Becky. "Thanks, you guys are great. I like you guys so much more."

"Well, Grace, we're not as cool as the other kids," Dallas said, looking down at her feet.

"Do you think I care? They're mean. I don't like them."

"Grace, just because they're mean, doesn't mean we have to be mean back."

"Sorry, Becky, you're right, but I get so mad sometimes."

"I know." Sighing, Becky sat on the floor, and we all joined her.

"I know we all just started to be friends, but I feel like I can really talk to you guys." As she looked around at each of us, she added, "I've never had friends before. Sure, I go to school with a lot of kids, but none of them have ever wanted to be friends with me." She then started to play with the string of her sweatshirt. I noticed it was a habit she did whenever she was nervous.

"I know I'm overweight. I'm reminded of it a lot by other kids. Sometimes as they walk by me, they snicker or laugh. Other times, they will mumble something under their breath so only I can hear. They will chant, '*fatty, fatty, two by four....*' or they make pig noises at me."

Whoa, this got serious really quick. I realized she must really need to talk to someone, but I found myself feeling uncomfortable the more I heard what people had done to her, but she continued.

"My mom came in my room one day and found me holding my phone, crying. I tried to sit up and hide it, but she grabbed it out of my hand before I could put it under my pillow. She scrolled down to see what was making me so sad."

I was so scared by then, because I knew it probably had to do with my friends. She lifted her sad eyes towards me and continued, "There was a text from Holly and Amy asking why I even exist. I remember it word for word. *'Hey fatty, did you eat the whole bakery section at the store on the way to school? Don't you realize donuts don't help your figure AT ALL! LOL. Seriously, I don't know why you even want to live. If I looked like you I would kill myself!' JK.*"

 The tree house was now the quietest I had ever heard it. All I could hear were the leaves rustling from the wind. Then one by one, tears started to roll down Becky's cheeks. I thought it was raining out because my hands started to have droplets hit them. But as I lifted my hands to my cheeks, I realized they were my own tears falling down my face. I blinked several times

and saw that there was not a dry eye in the tree house. Before Becky could say anything else, she was surrounded by hugs from all of us.

Words were expressed through tears of how beautiful she was, how special, and loved she was. As everyone finally sat back, Becky buried her face in her hands and just sobbed. Grace ran down the tree house ladder and came back with five rolls of toilet paper and handed one to each of us.

As I looked at my sister, I gave her a faint smile and winked. Boy, did I finally realize how much I loved her. My friends and I really had been jerks to her over the years. Tonight, I would have a long talk with her and tell her how sorry I was.

Dallas quietly started talking, "Becky, I know how it feels to be called names and picked on. Let me tell you something my mom reminds me of whenever I am being bullied or having a hard time with it. She says sometimes kids bully, trying to act all tough and want to say things to hurt you because they're jealous."

"Ha! That may be the case with some people but look at me. They are right, I am so much bigger than all of you. There is NOTHING they would ever be jealous of when it comes to me."

"Well, you always have a smile on your face and seem happy all the time. They're probably wanting that joy you always seem to have. It probably frustrates them to see you so happy when they think happiness comes from looking pretty and having nice clothes. My mom also says that bullies look for people they think are 'weak' or not tough because they won't fight back. She told me it's the 'sweethearts' in life that get bullied, but it isn't a weakness, it's caring. People who care about others and wouldn't want to hurt anyone else are very special people. They have a heart for love and peace, but they aren't going to be as 'cool' or seem as 'tough' as the others. She tells me *'Dallas, don't listen to those kids, they don't even know you. Their hearts are full of hate, pride, and arrogance. Keep your heart full of love, grace, and always stay humble. You have a special heart, others just don't see it, but I do."* Sighing as she wiped a tear, Dallas added, "I've never told anybody this, but I have cancer."

Gasps went around the room, except I already knew from my vision. Everyone started to talk at once, but Dallas put her hand up to silence us. "I am in remission, but that's why my hair is so short."

We all looked at her with blank faces. Then Grace asked, "What does remission mean?"

"Oh, sorry guys. My mom says it means my cancer is gone."

"Wow! That's great!" Becky said.

"Thanks. I will say, though, that lying in the hospital gave me a lot of time to think. I thought about if I really wanted to live and fight through this or not. Then I would always remember what my mom would say, and as I met other kids in the hospital, I realized I did care about others. There was a very sick little three-year-old girl in the hospital whose name was Mercy. She was a couple rooms down the hall from me. Getting to know her, I saw how loving and happy she was, even when she was so sick. She was very beautiful." She then paused, "She looked like an angel to me, with her blue eyes, fair skin while wearing white lacy pajamas. They were her favorite, so the hospital let her wear them. Her heart was so full of happiness and love that everyone that went into her room couldn't help but leave with a full heart. One day, I went to her room, and I sat in my wheelchair right by her tiny bed. She had become very weak, but she held her little hand out to me. I slowly pulled myself up and leaned over to hear what she had wanted to say to me.

"Your pretty, like a princess," she whispered out.

Then her hand dropped, and she closed her eyes and said so quietly I had to strain to hear her.

"I love you my princess."

I then rubbed her pale little cheek and told her I loved her back.

Tears started running down Dallas's face again as she continued, "Then just last week, my mom came into my room and sat on my bed. She told me that Mercy is now singing and dancing with the angels."

She was now looking straight at Becky and grabbed her hand. She then continued, "Please don't listen to those hurtful words, they are so not true. That little girl taught me where a person is truly beautiful. It has nothing to do with what color skin, hair, body shape, or size a person is. It comes from within. And Becky, the more I get to know you and the kindness and joy you express, the more you remind me of Mercy. You are beautiful and don't ever forget it."

Then, I watched as Dallas and Becky hugged and shed more tears. Man, were we going through a lot of toilet paper!

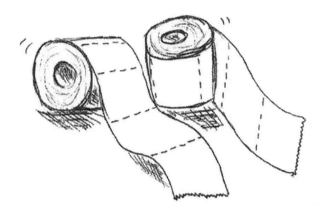

After the crying had stopped and we were all sitting in the circle again, I heard Tyler clear his throat.

"Um, Becky and Dallas? I am so sorry you've gone through so much. My story is different from both of yours, but it's still been hard on me. As you can see, I am very small for my age. I don't know why, but the bigger guys think that gives them the right to pick on me. My mom told me that kids will pick on others if they are 'different' in any way. She would say, *'if you're too tall, short, big, small, red hair, short hair, skin color, ANYTHING that is different from the others, they will find a reason to tease.'*"

Shaking his head, he continued, "Anyways, I've gotten beat up at recess, had a kid twist my ear and make me do things for him. I've had the bullies lie about me to get me in trouble."

He then looked at Dallas and Becky. "I've gotten a lot of texts too. I hate getting those. Sometimes they don't seem to stop!"

He then paused and looked down at his hands and added, "Then on top of that, last year my dad left my mom and me." Playing with the toilet paper roll, he added sadly, "My mom, who was usually so happy, got really sad for a long time. She quit going to work and would stay in her room all day and night. We didn't lose our house because my grandma helped pay our bills, but I had to take over everything at home, and I'm only thirteen.

Every time grandma came over, she brought us a warm meal and then would give me forty dollars to get food for the week. She said she'd give more but didn't have any more to give. So, every morning in the summer, I would ride my bike to the store because they would give out free breakfast and drinks. I would grab my mom and me a donut and then grab a chocolate milk for me and a coffee for her, and that would be our breakfast. Then during the school year, I always skipped lunch and brought it home to split it with her."

"Oh my gosh, Tyler. What about dinner?" Grace asked wide-eyed.

"Dinner? Um, if I ran out of the forty dollars before grandma came again, we would go without dinner, or I would pop up some popcorn or macaroni and cheese if I had any in the house."

"Is it still that way at home now?"

"No, for a couple weeks now, my mom has been doing so much better. She even got her old job back at the hospital. She's a nurse," he said with a little pride, and you could see him sit a little taller.

"Oh, that's great. How did she get her job back if she doesn't leave her room?" Becky asked while she continued wiping tears.

"Well, the craziest thing happened. A couple of weeks ago, my mom and I were home, and I heard our doorbell ring. I went to answer it, and there were bags of food for us sitting on the porch. I couldn't believe it. We hadn't had that much food in our house since my dad left us!"

"How did that change your mom?" I asked, curious to know how something we did could have helped so much.

"Well, it had gotten pretty bad. We hadn't had dinner the night before, and we were hungry. The day the food came, my mom hadn't even been out of bed yet. When she saw all the food, she realized how bad she had gotten."

"Oh my gosh, we're so happy for you! So glad your mom is doing better. Do you guys need any help with anything?"

"No thanks, Cat, and we're really doing so much better. My mom keeps walking around the house smiling and saying, 'We have food and shelter, but most of all we have a home full of love.' Then she comes over and hugs me all the time now." Looking sheepishly down at his lap, he added, "I kind of like it when she does that, because she was so sad for so long, that I love when she smiles."

"Of course. That's great! So glad your mom is happy again."

Smiling, he thanked us.

"Well, this has been the saddest but coolest time I have ever had in my tree house. Thank you, guys, for sharing. How about we end this with a bowl of ice cream!"

With a whole bunch of "Yea's," we all rushed back to the house to enjoy a treat.

CHAPTER 18

Friday had finally arrived, and we were all so excited. Well, almost everyone. I looked over and saw Holly, Amy, and Tiffany not helping decorate for the party. They all just stood out in the hallway in a huddle together, whispering about something.

Wondering what they were up to, I walked over to them and asked, "Hey guys, are you wanting to help?"

"Are you kidding, why would we help? The party is for the poor kids. Gross, why would we help with that?" Holly answered with a sneer on her face.

"Yeah, Cat, we really thought you were cooler than this." Amy added looking around the room.

I just stood there with my mouth hanging open. I didn't even know what to say.

"Well, I . . . uh, we . . . "I couldn't get any words out. Then finally, I heard myself say, "I thought you were all my friends."

"Ha!" Holly yelled. "You sure haven't acted like a friend to us! You've been a jerk, and we are starting to think that you're no better than those new loser friends you're now hanging out with."

I've never had my friends talk bad about me. I've actually never had anyone call me anything mean before. I now got just a tiny glimpse of what Becky, Tyler, and Dallas had been going through. So, I lost it and snapped at them. "Stop it!" Trying not to yell, because I didn't want anyone else to hear, I answered in my just-below-yelling voice, "You guys have it all wrong. You don't know what true friends really are."

"No, *you* don't know what real friends are. Real friends don't put others before their besties," Holly replied.

"That is where you're wrong. Real friends don't hurt each other, or other people, and that's what you do."

I then turned and walked away as a tear slid down my cheek. Right then, Dallas walked up to me. "Hey Cat, I heard all of that." She then paused. "I've never had anyone stick up for me before. I just wanted to say thank you.

I know that had to have been very hard for you." Then looking down at her feet, she added, "And I just wanted to say I'm sorry."

"For what?"

"I'm sorry for that day I said I thought you were being nice to me because of a dare. I now realize you really were trying to be my friend."

"That's okay, Dallas." I gave her a half smile. "I see now why you would've thought that of me. I really was a jerk. I should be the one saying sorry."

"Ah, don't worry about it." She nodded her head towards the door. "Let's go check on everyone to see how far they've gotten."

Smiling, we walked down the hall and sped up as we heard tons of laughter coming from the cafeteria.

"Beat yah there!" And the next thing I knew, Dallas was running full speed down the hall.

CHAPTER 19

Waking up, I jumped out of bed. Today's the day! Today's the day of the sale. I couldn't wait to get started!

"Cat! Are you ready? Today's Saturday!" Grace yelled as she jumped onto my bed. I could see she was already dressed in a pair of jeans and a mint green sweater. She was all ready for the day.

I then grabbed my jeans and my favorite grey hooded sweatshirt. I hurried into the bathroom and knew that Grace must have just gotten done with a shower, because the mirror was all fogged up. I grabbed my sleeve and wiped the steam off the mirror. To my horror I saw my reflection! My hair was sticking out every which way, and my pajamas were twisted all around me.

"Whoa, holy cow!" I said out loud. I turned to see Grace had followed me and I had never answered her. "Um Grace, do I look ready?" I answered as I turned her way and pointed to my hair.

"Um, no, not really, but hurry up! Just throw your hair up in a pony tail. I can't wait to get started! It's going to be a good day!"

"Grace, it's only seven o'clock in the morning. We can't get there until eight."

"That's alright. I'll go get us some breakfast." And out the bathroom door she flew.

As I heard her run down the steps, I grabbed my brush, and with a sigh, I began the one thing I hated to do every morning. Brush my crazy, snarled hair. Grace was right. Today was a good day. A good day to wear my hair up in a pony tail.

***

"So," Grace started as we sat and began to eat toast and cereal. "When we get there, everything should be set up already, right? We just have to put the food out?"

"Yup. I can't believe how many people are helping us. Last night, we had a lot of help putting up the tables and sorting through the clothes and toys."

"I know, and today your whole class is coming to help!"

Pushing my cereal around with my spoon, I sighed. "Yeah, all but Holly, Amy, and Tiff. They told me the idea was stupid and there was no way they'd show up to something that Becky, Tyler, and Dallas were a part of. Then they looked at me and said 'We thought you were cooler than this, Cat! If you are going to keep hanging out with those losers, then we will not be your friends anymore. Your choice.'"

"No way! That's so mean!"

Sadly, I had to agree with my sister.

"Cat, I bet it was Holly who said that wasn't it?"

"Yeah, but Amy was smiling along with Holly. Only Tiff looked a little sad."

"Well, I'd tell you who I would choose, but I think you already know."

"I know," I responded, taking a bite of my favorite toast, cinnamon and sugar. Slowly, I chewed to enjoy every last bite then swallowed and added, "I just didn't think I'd have to 'choose' between them. I mean, can't I be friends with all of them?"

"Well, I don't see Becky, Dallas or Tyler acting like that. I think it's kind of sick that the others are making you choose. I don't think that's a good friend."

"I know, it's just that we've been friends for so long. How can they just stop being my friend, just like that?" I snapped my fingers as my voice squeaked because I was on the verge of tears.

"All I know, sis, is that today is supposed to be a fun day. We're doing something good to help others and have fun at the same time. Don't let them ruin your day. Remember what mom has said before." She tilted her head the way our mom always does, and she said in a voice as close to our moms as possible. *"Kids can be so mean. Remember, Cat and Grace, you are no better than the geekiest kids in school, but the most popular kids are no better than you. Be kind to everyone."*

Smiling, I got up and gave my sister a hug. "How did you get so smart?"

Grinning, she shrugged out of my arms and said, "I learned from my big sis."

"Hmph, hardly," I mumbled. "I've been the mean one. But you're right.

They're no better than Becky, Dallas, Tyler, or us! If they don't want to be my friend, then that's their choice."

"Yes, their choice, but their loss too. They'll be losing a great friend."

Realizing this conversation was getting way too serious for a day that was supposed to be fun, I added, "Okay, let's stop talking about all this sad stuff. You're right. Let's go have some fun!"

"Now you're talking!"

We then began to load up all the brownies, cookies, and other goodies we had made as my mom walked into the kitchen. "Good morning girls, I see you're up and ready."

"Yeah, as soon as you're ready, Mom, can we go?"

"Sure." As she stretched out her arms and yawned, she added, "Just let me get my cup of coffee, and we'll be on our way."

"Great! We're all set."

"Did you remember the punch, girls?"

"Dallas is going to bring it, but we've got the cups."

"Great. Just give me ten minutes and we'll be on our way."

"Okay, are you going to buy anything today?"

As she held her steaming cup of coffee, she said, "Hmm, let me see. I've had two very excited girls working hard nonstop for weeks now on this sale. Of course, I'm going to buy something. The whole thing is a great idea. What time does the sale actually start?"

"Nine o'clock!"

"Then that means your dad and I will be at the doors no later than 9:30. The first thing we'll buy is a certain person's special brownie for me and a cookie for your dad, to go with our coffee."

Grace pulled out one of her brownies she had made, and grinned. "You can eat one now if you promise to buy one later too."

"Wow, you sure drive a hard bargain," she mumbled as she slowly chewed on the brownie.

Laughing, we finished loading up the car and headed to the school. I couldn't wait! Today was going to be so much fun! Nothing, I mean nothing, was going to ruin my day. As my mom drove, I looked out the window at the bare trees. I could see all the leaves on the ground now. It was a beautiful day. The sun was shining and there were yellow, red, and orange leaves laying like a blanket all over the ground. I couldn't stop thinking that this was going to be a perfect day. What could possibly go wrong?

CHAPTER 20

As we entered the school with our arms fully loaded, I could see Becky and Dallas already there.

I stopped to take a look around the room. Balloons and streamers were hanging all around the cafeteria. Smiling to myself I remembered the look on Tyler's face when Becky insisted on pink and yellow. Tyler didn't say anything, but we could all tell he wasn't real excited about the color choices.

I could also hear music in the back ground, and the tables were full of clothes and toys that were donated by so many people. It really looked great.

"Guys! Aren't you so excited?"

Laughing at Becky's excitement, I responded, "Yeah, we can't wait to get started. A lot of our class should be

here soon to help."

"Great! Dallas just made the punch and put it on the table, you can add all the treats right next to it."

Walking over to Dallas I asked, "What kind of punch did you make?"

"It has red juice with vanilla ice cream and a clear pop poured into it. I can't wait for everyone to try it." Then she looked down at her feet and shyly added, "I hope you all like it."

"Good, I'll try some in a little bit."

"Okay, girls," I heard my mom say. I'd forgotten she was standing next to me, holding the box of treats. "Where do you want me to set these?"

"Oh, in the kitchen, and we'll put them on plates. Thanks, Mom."

"No problem. Looking around the room, she added, "I'm very proud of you all for doing this. I know it's been a lot of work."

"Thanks, but a lot of fun too!"

"Yes, Grace, a lot of fun too. Now, I'm going to head out and get your father. I'll be back after it opens. I've got to try that punch." Winking, she started to walk off, only to hear Grace yell after her, "And a brownie Mom!"

"Oh, yes." She stopped and turned around. "Of course, and a brownie."

***

Nine o'clock came before we knew it. Our whole class was there, well almost. My old 'friends' were the only ones missing.

"Hey, guys, we've got a long line outside waiting to come in!"

"That's great Tyler. Is Mrs. Hill going to let them in now?"

"Yup, let's all get to our stations," he added, grinning.

Dallas and Grace were going to work the food and drink table. Tyler was really good with math, so he was going to be in charge of the money box, while Becky and I sat with him and bagged up everything people bought.

The morning had been going just great. Boy, were we selling a lot of stuff, but all of a sudden, we heard some screaming from the hallway.

We all took off to see what was going on, and that was our biggest mistake. Because when we all left the cafeteria that was when the trouble began.

As we reached the hall, there sat Amy on the floor, grabbing her ankle, while Tiffany rolled her eyes.

I stood there with my mouth hanging open. "What are you guys doing here? You said you weren't coming." I bit my tongue from saying anything more because it wouldn't be nice.

Moaning, Amy whimpered. "We were just coming to see how the sale was going, but I tripped and twisted my ankle."

I looked at Tiffany, and she just shrugged her shoulders and mumbled, "I didn't see it happen." Then she looked down at the ground. Probably so she wouldn't have to look at me. Man, did they hate me that much?

People started to walk back into the cafeteria when they realized it was nothing serious. I couldn't put my finger on it, but something just didn't feel right. I could feel it in my stomach. Shaking my head back and forth, I realized what it was.

"Hey, where's Holly?" I knew Amy would never leave Holly's side.

With a sing song voice, I heard behind me, "Did somebody say my name?"

Taking a deep breath and clenching my fists together, I tried to stay calm. I slowly turned around and Holly gave me one of her fake smiles.

"Well, girls, there really isn't anything worth buying in there. Let's get going."

Before I realized what was happening, Amy was up and practically running to keep up with Holly. Something was really wrong here. Amy's ankle sure got better quickly.

As they were going out the door in a rush, Tiffany turned around and looked at me with a frown and mouthed, "Sorry." She then ran out the door, and they all jumped on their bikes.

Sorry? For what, I wondered. Boy, it sure didn't take me long to figure out why she'd said that. As I walked back into the cafeteria, I heard a boy yelling, "Gross! Yuck!" I looked closer, and he was holding one of Grace's brownies in his hand. Grace and Dallas's eyes were huge.

CHAPTER 21

"What? What's wrong?" Grace exclaimed.

"Drink! Mom get me a drink!" The little boy's mom grabbed the cup of punch Dallas had poured them.

"Here son, drink this." The boy took a drink and grabbed his throat and started screaming. His mom was now on her knees trying to figure out what was going on.

"What, honey, what's wrong?"

By now, the boy had tears streaming down his cheeks and his face was beet red.

The boy's mom grabbed another cup of punch from the table and took a swig. "Ugh!" She then turned and looked straight at Dallas and Grace. "What is wrong with you girls! You can't serve this punch! It's burning my throat! And my sons!"

She then grabbed her son and ran out of the cafeteria to find a drinking fountain. I ran over and grabbed a brownie and took a bite. "Ugh, disgusting!" I yelled and ran over to the trash can to spit it out. Then I grabbed a drink to see what the lady had been talking about. "Hot! Hot!" I hollered.

By then Grace and Dallas had lost it. They took off sobbing and ran out of the room.

"Cat, what's wrong?" Becky asked as she started pounding on my back. Now everyone in the room was looking at us.

"Hot!" I tried to say. Then I choked out, "Get that food and punch out of here!"

Tyler, Becky, and some others from my class started hauling all the food back into the kitchen. I turned back around to see most people were putting their items that were in their arms back on the table and leaving.

"No!" I tried to yell. "Don't go!" But the words failed to come out. I just sounded like a croaking frog.

My mom and teacher were by my side. "What is it, Cat? What's wrong?"

By now, I had tears running down my face. After a few minutes, I was able to say, "Garlic and hot sauce."

Mom and Mrs. Hill looked at each other, then back at me, "What honey?"

"Mom, the brownies are covered in garlic, and there was something hot in the punch!"

By now my whole class was staring at me with faces full of shock. Tyler ran over to the trash can and dug

around inside of it. Then he pulled out a large bottle of hot sauce and a shaker of garlic powder.

"I don't understand, Cat, why would Grace and Dallas do that?"

Then it hit me. Amy's fake sprained ankle, Holly's not so real smile as she came out of the cafeteria, and Tiffany's 'sorry'.

"They wouldn't Mom, but I know who would!" I then lost it again. Knowing what they did sent me into another round of sobs, my tears were running as fast as a waterfall. They had just ruined our big day, and why? Because they didn't like my new friends.

Bullying? This was far more dangerous than talking about others behind their backs in a treehouse. They could have seriously hurt that boy. No, I realized even talking about others behind their backs was very dangerous. Look at how it had affected Becky, Dallas, and Tyler. My tears had slowed to just a gentle drip now, and I was filled with anger. I was mad, no make that furious!

"Cat, Cat, honey, what is it?"

"Mom, can you see if there are any snacks left and punch that are still good to put out?"

"I sure can."

"And Mrs. Hill, can you get everyone back in their areas and we can get selling again? This is a good cause, and I'm not letting others meanness ruin our day."

My teacher put her hand on my shoulder and smiled. "Definitely Cat, you' re right. Let's get this sale running again."

I watched her take off as I did the same, only in the opposite direction. I was on my way to find Grace and Dallas, when I spotted them in the hall. Grace was rubbing Dallas's back telling her it was okay. I plopped myself down on the ground next to them.

"Sorry, guys." I heard myself say.

"Sorry?" They both looked at me.

"You didn't do anything wrong. They just didn't like our food." Dallas cried.

I realized that they didn't know what had happened. They thought the boy and his mom just didn't like their punch and brownies. I looked at Dallas to explain, but her red puffy eyes met mine, and I started to see stars. "Oh boy," I thought, "here it comes again."

I saw Dallas at her kitchen counter earlier this morning with all her ingredients for the punch bowl.

"But what if I mess up, Mom? I've never made this before."

"Honey, what's wrong? It's so easy. You just throw all the stuff into the bowl when you get there and stir. That simple. Everyone will love it."

Shaking her head back and forth, Dallas cried more to herself than to her mom. "But what if I mess up? What if they don't like it?"

"Dallas, sweetheart, look at me." She looked up at her mom. "What are you afraid of?"

Then a tear slid down her cheek. "If I mess up," she choked out, "my

new friends might not like me anymore."

I shook my head to clear the vision. Did Dallas really think we wouldn't like her if we didn't like her punch?

"Um, sis, you okay?" I heard Grace ask.

"Yeah." Then I realized I had to tell them it was not their fault. "Guys, you didn't do anything wrong." Then I went into all the details of how Amy, Holly, and Tiffany had set them up.

"What?" Grace was now on her feet. "Why would they do that?" But I was still focused on Dallas.

"Dallas, you didn't ruin the punch. Holly did. I tasted it before she did anything to it, and I think it was the best punch I've ever tasted! And you know what? My mom and Becky are in the kitchen right now trying to make more, but I think they need your help, because you make the best punch."

Smiling, Dallas jumped to her feet. "You think so? Thanks, Cat!" and she ran off.

I called after her, "Hey Dallas!"

Slowing, she turned, "Yeah?"

"Even if you had the worst tasting punch, you're still a great friend."

Smiling, she gave me a nod and headed back into the cafeteria.

"You had one of those vision things, didn't you? I saw your eyes do something funny."

"Yeah, I did, Grace, but let's not worry about that right now. Let's go finish our sale."

Walking back into the cafeteria, I only half listened to my sister rant on about giving Holly a piece of her mind.

Chapter 22

The rest of the day went without any more upsets. When the sale was over, Mrs. Hill added up all the money we had made, and it totaled over $2000! It was all going to go towards meals, backpacks, and clothes for kids in our school that had those types of needs.

I went and found a chair in the corner of the room. I just had to rest a second before I started cleaning up. I looked around and saw Dallas and Grace putting the food away. They were sneaking broken pieces of the cookies and brownies into their mouths and laughing. Looking closer, I realized it was Dallas laughing while Grace's mouth moved a mile a minute, even with food stuffed in it.

Smiling, I then looked and saw Becky grinning and talking with Mrs. Hill. Becky's arms were just a flaring as she talked. She always had a smile on her face, but the more I got to know her, the more I realized she had two types of smiles. One that she used whenever she was trying to hide the pain and hurt of others. I now recognized it as her 'fake' or 'show' smile. As I watched her now, I could see it was a totally different smile. It was one that lit up her whole entire face. There was no fakeness about it. It was a full-fledged genuine smile that made her whole face glow.

Then there was Tyler. He was a trooper being the only boy in our group. I sat there watching him help fold up the tables with other kids in our class, smiling as the others chatted away. He may be smaller than some of the other kids, but he was always so nice and patient with everyone. He really had become a great friend to all of us.

Tiffany had texted me an hour after they had left to apologize for what they had done. She wanted to still be my friend. I would have to get together with her and have a long talk about it, because one thing I knew for sure was that these new friends of mine would stay my friends. Also, I was going to try to not be mean anymore. My days of bullying were over.

As I looked around, I saw Mr. Williams, our very *old* janitor. All the kids, (me included) had always called him 'One-Eyed, Scar Face'. He had a patch over one eye, and a huge scar that ran down the same side of his face. Everyone, I mean *everyone* had always been so scared of him. I sat there and watched as he started to slowly shuffle from table to table. He then dropped his cleaning rag onto the floor. Now my old self would have sat there and watched him try to pick it up. But before he could lean down to retrieve it, I jumped out of my seat and yelled out, "I got it for you, Mr. Williams." I rushed over to help the old, frail, grey-haired man.

Grabbing the rag off the floor I straightened up and reached out to hand it back to him.

"Thanks so much," he whispered faintly, giving me a strained half smile. Then his one eye connected with my set of eyes and I started to see stars...

If you enjoyed reading I AM "NOT" A BULLY by Paula Range then watch for the next book in the Vision Series:

COMING SOON IN FALL OF 2019:

Book #2 - I AM A TREASURE SEEKER by Paula Range

To find when the next book will be released please visit me on Facebook at:

www.facebook.com/paularangeauthor

Feel free to leave a review on Amazon to tell me what you think about Cat and her friends!

NOTE FROM THE AUTHOR

One thing I always tell my kids, just like in the book:

Think of a kid in your school who is the 'geekiest' or 'weirdest'. Know this: You are no better than them.

But now think of the most popular kid(s) in your school and know this: They are no better than you.

Everyone needs a friend.

Be kind to each other, even if they are different than you.

Different does not mean bad or weird.

See the beauty in being different. Life would be boring if we were all the same.

ABOUT THE AUTHOR

Paula Range lives in the Midwest with her husband, and five children. After being a stay at home mom for 18 years, she has started her love for writing children's books. When she isn't writing she goes on walks with her family or is busy driving them to events.

Made in the USA
Monee, IL
14 January 2020